MOON

MO

ON

ALISON OLIVER

CLARION BOOKS | Houghton Mifflin Harcourt | Boston New York

CLARION BOOKS
3 Park Avenue
New York, New York 10016

Clarion Books is an imprint of Houghton Mifflin Harcourt Publishing Company.

www.hmhco.com

The illustrations in this book were executed in watercolor, brush pen,
charcoal, and potato stamp, and assembled digitally.
The text was set in M Twentieth Century.

Library of Congress Cataloging-in-Publication Data
Names: Oliver, Alison, author. Title: Moon / Alison Oliver.
Description: Boston ; New York : Houghton Mifflin Harcourt, [2018] |
Summary: Throughout her busy days, Moon wonders what it would be like to be
wild and free until the day she meets a wolf and learns his "wolfy ways."
Identifiers: LCCN 2017020189 | ISBN 9781328781604 (hardcover)
Subjects: | CYAC: Freedom—Fiction. | Wolves—Fiction.
Classification: LCC PZ7.1.O459 Moo 2018 | DDC [E]—dc23
LC record available at https://lccn.loc.gov/2017020189

Manufactured in China
SCP 10 9 8 7 6 5 4 3 2 1
4500692585

To Louanne,
for keeping me wild

Every day, Moon walked home
from school and thought about
the day.

There was always a lot to do.

Moon always did it all.
But she wondered what it
would be like not to.

What would it feel like to be free?
To run. To yell. To be wild. Can you learn to be wild?
Moon couldn't find the answer anywhere.

That night, Moon saw a shooting star zip by.

She went outside to watch for more.

What she found was different—paw prints!
Strange.

Exciting.

Wild.

There, in the garden, a beautiful,
furry creature stared back at her.

A wolf.

Wolf offered Moon a ride.
In a flash they were off
to the edge of the Great Forest.

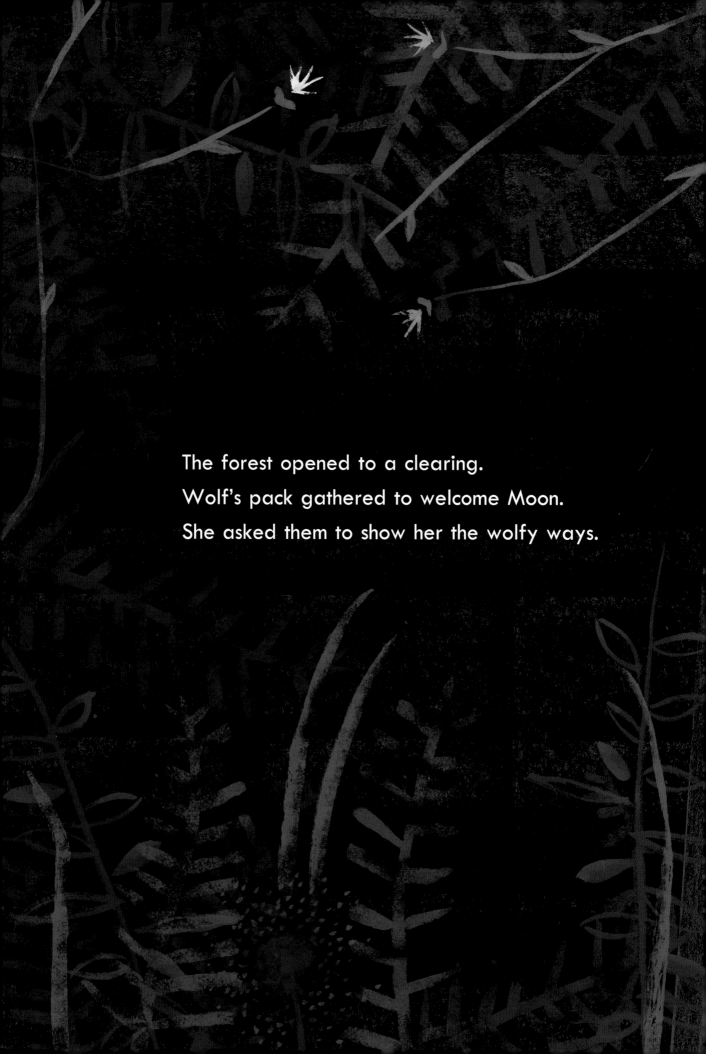

The forest opened to a clearing.
Wolf's pack gathered to welcome Moon.
She asked them to show her the wolfy ways.

How to pounce.

How to play.

How to howl.

How to be still,
how to listen and feel.

The breeze blew through Moon's hair.

The chirping of the insects seemed to grow quiet.

The ocean of stars felt not so far away.

The forest exhaled. And so did Moon.
It was wild.

Moon was happy.

Then she heard a howl—the familiar voice of her mother.
Moon knew she had to go home.

But she wasn't the same Moon anymore.

The next day, Moon
walked to school.

And she took her wolfy ways with her.